DISCARD

Daisy All-Sorts

VIKING

Published by the Penguin Group
Penguin Books Australia Ltd
250 Camberwell Road
Camberwell, Victoria 3124, Australia
Penguin Books Ltd
80 Strand, London WC3R ORL, England
Penguin Putnam Inc.
375 Hudson Street, New York, New York 10014, USA
Penguin Books Canada Limited
10 Alcorn Avenue, Toronto, Ontario, Canada, M4V 3B2
Penguin Books (N.Z.) Ltd
Cnr Rosedale and Airborne Roads, Albany, Auckland, New Zealand
Penguin Books (South Africa) (Pty) Ltd
24 Sturdee Avenue, Rosebank, Johannesburg 2196, South Africa
Penguin Books India (P) Ltd
11, Community Centre, Panchsheel Park, New Delhi, 110 017, India

First published by Penguin Books Australia, 2002

1 3 5 7 9 10 8 6 4 2

Designed by Deborah Brash, Penguin Design Studio
Typeset in New Astor
Colour separations by Splitting Image Colour Studio, Victoria
Printed and bound by Imago Productions, Singapore

National Library of Australia
Cataloguing-in-Publication data:

Allen, Pamela.
Daisy All-Sorts

ISBN 0 670 90302 7.

1. Dogs – Juvenile fiction. I. Title.

A823.3

www.puffin.com.au

Daisy All-Sorts

Pamela Allen

VIKING

For Bessie, Charlie, and Biddy of Whitianga
whose story this is.

Daisy was an ordinary dog.
Every day she went for an ordinary walk with Stanley.
Life had always been ordinary for as long as Stanley
and Daisy could remember.

But all that changed the day Stanley
bought himself a bicycle.
A beautiful brand new bicycle with
a beautiful brand new helmet.

He put on the helmet and buckled it under his chin.

He swung his leg high over the bar and called, 'DAYZEEEEEEEEEEEEEEEEE!'

And he was off down the hill.

Daisy ran fast, very fast,
but she couldn't keep up.

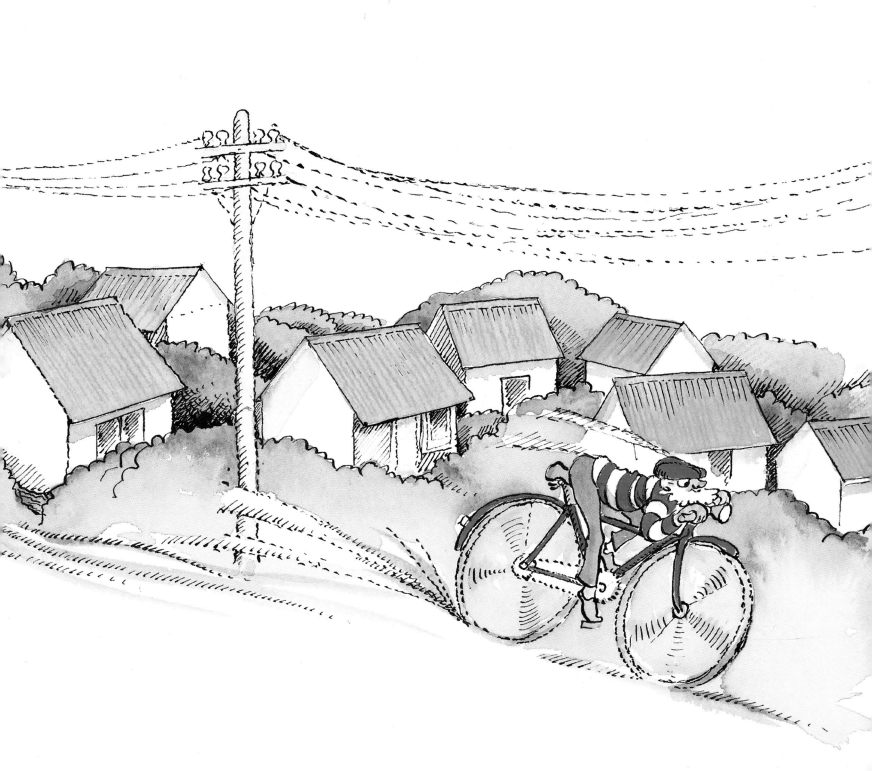

Stanley waited for her at the bottom of the hill,
and while he waited, Bella came out of her house
to admire his beautiful brand new bicycle
and his beautiful brand new helmet.

At last, hot and tired, Daisy arrived.
'You poor thing,' murmured Bella.
'Did you get left behind today?'
and she went inside for a bowl of water.
Then from deep down inside her pocket,
she pulled out
THREE LIQUORICE ALL-SORTS.

The next day, Stanley again waited
at the bottom of the hill.
When Daisy arrived, panting,
Bella gave her a bowl of water.
But this time there were NO liquorice all-sorts.

All Daisy could think of were liquorice all-sorts.
She flopped down and wagged her tail.
'That's very good,' said Bella.
'But I don't *have* any liquorice all-sorts today.'
Daisy wagged her tail harder than she had
ever wagged it before.

She tried every trick she knew.
She danced doggy dances,
she sang silly songs,

she barked, she bounced and she begged.
But Bella didn't *have* any liquorice all-sorts.

When Stanley was ready to go,
Daisy wouldn't come. Daisy was waiting,
hoping for at least one lovely little liquorice lolly.

'DAYZEEEEEEEEEEEEEEEE!' called Stanley.

He called and he coaxed.
He pushed and he pleaded.
He grumbled and he growled, 'DAY-ZEE!'

But Daisy wouldn't move.

At last, Stanley picked her up.
She was heavy, very heavy.

He placed her across the bar
of the beautiful brand new bicycle.

Then, huffing and puffing,
plodding and panting,
he wheeled her up the hill
and all the way home.

When they got home, Stanley was exhausted.

What was he going to do tomorrow?

When tomorrow came, Daisy started early.
She reached Bella's house long before Stanley.
All she could think about were lovely liquorice all-sorts.

'Please, Bella,' begged Daisy. 'Please?'
Bella gave her a bowl of water, as before,
but no liquorice all-sorts.

'I love you, Bella,' licked Daisy,
with lots of sticky licky love kisses.
But still there were no liquorice all-sorts.

Since yesterday's fuss, Bella had been thinking and when Stanley arrived she handed HIM a small brown paper bag.

'For Daisy when you get home,' she said.

'It's a surprise.'

This time, when Stanley waved good-bye,
there wasn't a problem,

because Daisy followed
the bag all the way home.

When they got home, Stanley gave her
the contents of the little brown paper bag
that Bella had given him.

What do you think was inside?

Not three, but FOUR liquorice all-sorts.

Daisy was so delighted, she danced doggy dances,
she sang silly songs, she barked, she bounced,
and when she was quite quite finished . . .

. . . she bowed.

After that, nothing was ever ordinary again.

Now, every day, Bella waits with a little brown paper bag, 'for Daisy', and every evening Daisy dances.

People come from far and wide to watch

'DAISY ALL-SORTS
THE EXTRAORDINARY
DANCING DOG'

and they clap, and they clap, and they clap.